THIS WALKER BOOK BELONGS TO:

_____

_____

_____

For Geraldine, Joe, Naomi, Eddie, Laura and Isaac
M.R.

For Elaine, Charlotte and Nicola
A.R.

First published 1990 by
Walker Books Ltd, 87 Vauxhall Walk
London SE11 5HJ

This edition published 1999

2 4 6 8 10 9 7 5 3

Text © 1990 Michael Rosen
Illustrations © 1990 Arthur Robins

Printed in Hong Kong

British Library Cataloguing in Publication Data
A catalogue record for this book is
available from the British Library.

ISBN 0-7445-6945-1

Little Rabbit Foo Foo

illustrated by
Arthur Robins

retold by
Michael Rosen

WALKER BOOKS
AND SUBSIDIARIES
LONDON • BOSTON • SYDNEY

Little Rabbit Foo Foo

riding through the forest,

scooping up the field mice

and bopping them on the head.

Down came the Good Fairy and said, "Little Rabbit Foo Foo, I don't like your attitude, scooping up the field mice and bopping them on the head. I'm going to give you three chances to change, and if you don't, I'm going to turn you into a goonie."

Little Rabbit Foo Foo
riding through the forest,

scooping up the wriggly worms
and bopping them on the head.

Down came the Good Fairy

and said, "Little Rabbit Foo Foo, I don't like your attitude, scooping up the wriggly worms and bopping them on the head. You've got two chances to change, and if you don't, I'm going to turn you into a goonie."

Little Rabbit Foo Foo
riding through the forest,
scooping up the tigers
and bopping them on the head.

Down came the Good Fairy
and said, "Little Rabbit Foo Foo,
I don't like your attitude,
scooping up the tigers
and bopping them on the head.

"You've got one chance left to change,
and if you don't, I'm going to
turn you into a goonie."

Little Rabbit Foo Foo
riding through the forest,
scooping up the goblins

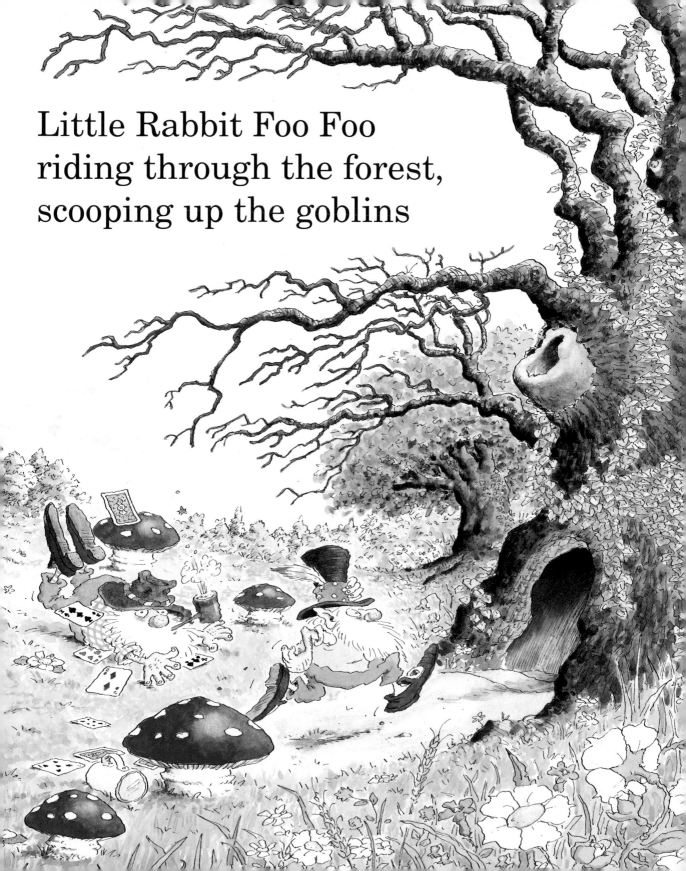

and bopping them on the head.

Down came the Good Fairy
and said, "Little Rabbit Foo Foo,
I don't like your attitude,
scooping up the goblins
and bopping them on the head.

"You've got no chances left, so I'm
going to turn you into a goonie."

MORE WALKER PAPERBACKS
For You to Enjoy

THIS IS OUR HOUSE
Michael Rosen/Bob Graham

George says the cardboard house is his and no one else can play with it.
But Lindy, Marly, Freddie, Charlene, Marlene, Luther, Sophie and Rasheda have other ideas!

"Michael Rosen and Bob Graham have created a picture book that is a
pleasure to share." *The School Librarian*

0-7445-6020-9   £4.99

WE'RE GOING ON A BEAR HUNT
Michael Rosen/Helen Oxenbury

Winner of the Smarties Book Prize and Highly Commended for the Kate Greenaway Medal

"A dramatic and comic masterpiece… Beautifully produced, written and illustrated,
this is a classic." *The Independent on Sunday*

0-7445-2323-0   £4.99

THE MAGIC BICYCLE
Brian Patten/Arthur Robins

When young Danny Harris knocks a witch into a ditch, she puts a spell on his
bike that sends him off on an amazing journey around the world!

"Packed with jokes and buzzing with life." *The Mail on Sunday*

0-7445-3651-0   £4.99

Walker Paperbacks are available from most booksellers, or by post from B.B.C.S., P.O. Box 941, Hull, North Humberside HU1 3YQ

24 hour telephone credit card line 01482 224626

To order, send: Title, author, ISBN number and price for each book ordered, your full name and address,
cheque or postal order payable to BBCS for the total amount and allow the following for postage and packing:
UK and BFPO: £1.00 for the first book, and 50p for each additional book to a maximum of £3.50.
Overseas and Eire: £2.00 for the first book, £1.00 for the second and 50p for each additional book.

Prices and availability are subject to change without notice.